Mrs May was ill.
The children had a new teacher.
He was called Mr Fry.

It was story time.
The children sat in the
reading corner.

Mr Fry had a new story.
The story was about a king.
He was called King Arthur.

'Here is King Arthur,' said Mr Fry,
'and here are his knights.
They lived a long time ago.'

King Arthur had a round table.
All the knights sat round it.
They liked the round table.

The children did a project.
The boys were knights.
'It's not fair,' said Biff.

Biff wanted to be a knight.
'It's not fair,' she said.
'Why can't girls be knights?'

Biff was in her room.
She wanted to go skateboarding.
But the magic key began to glow.

‘Oh blow!’ said Biff.
‘I wanted to go skateboarding.’

The magic took Biff to
King Arthur's castle.
It put her in a dress.

‘Yuk!’ said Biff.
‘I wanted to be a knight.
Knights don’t wear dresses.’

Biff was cross with the magic.
She saw some knights.
'Can I be a knight?' she said.

The knights laughed.
'But you are a girl,' they said.
'Girls can't be knights.'

Biff got on her skateboard.
'You couldn't do that,' she said.
'Now can I be a knight?'

The knights were amazed.
'We'll have to ask King
Arthur,' said the knights.

The knights took Biff to King Arthur.
'This is Biff,' they said.
'She wants to be a knight.'

King Arthur laughed.
'Girls can't be knights,' he said.
'Why not?' asked Biff.

King Arthur called a meeting but
the knights argued.

No-one wanted to sit down.
They all wanted to sit near
King Arthur.

Biff had a good idea.
She spoke to King Arthur.
'Get a round table,' she said.

The knights liked the round table.
'It's brilliant!' they said.
'Now we won't argue.'

The knights sat round the table.
'See!' said Biff.
'Now can I be a knight?'

But everyone laughed.
'I'm sorry,' said King Arthur,
'but girls can't be knights.'

The magic adventure was over.
'It's not fair,' said Biff.
'Girls are as good as boys.'